DESIRE PATH

PITT POETRY SERIES

Nancy Krygowski and Jeffrey McDaniel, *Editors*

DESIRE PATH

Winner of the Agnes Lynch Starrett Poetry Prize

MIGWI MWANGI

Published by the University of Pittsburgh Press, Pittsburgh, Pa., 15260

Manufactured in the United States of America
Printed on acid-free paper
10 9 8 7 6 5 4 3 2 1

ISBN 13: 978-0-8229-6834-4
ISBN 10: 0-8229-6834-7

Cover art: Wangari Mathenge, *Ascendants VI (Imperial Reckoning)*, 2020. Oil on canvas, 68 x 90 in. © Wangari Mathenge. Courtesy of Roberts Projects, Los Angeles, California. Photo Brian Griffin.

Cover and book design by Alex Wolfe

Publisher: University of Pittsburgh Press, 7500 Thomas Blvd., 4th floor, Pittsburgh, PA 15260, United States, www.upittpress.org

EU Authorized Representative: Easy Access System Europe, Mustamäe tee 50, 10621 Tallinn, Estonia, gpsr.requests@easproject.com

CONTENTS

V

Never mind that
no kingdom was ever won

by small gestures

—CARL PHILLIPS

Eros is a verb

—ANNE CARSON

TO SPOON WITH YOU

To spoon or be spooned?
Two bodies side to side.

To curl or be curled into?
The heat of a hand on your chest or waist.

Each night finding reason to trace
the other's nearest rhythms:
scalpscent of dandruff Vatika

sudden as an involuntary jerk, a ripple in
the tether of unknowable dreams.

Across New York, our borrowed city,
helicopters occupy the stars. Floodlights
scavenge for keffiyehs, tents cobbled

overcrowded avenues. To tend,
this late hour, you
so-finished, drooling the pillowcase

or release & turn
attendant to my own numbed strain?

Across our nonresident state,
teams of armored officers slice
same-day shipments: heavy-duty zip ties.

Our nonimmigrant states, a sea
of double-locking
self-locking parentheses

& here, now, by luck?
Silence of near sleep.

Above us, the landlord's flushed toilet
throats farts, spent tissues
through the off-white walls

to a lightless city
beaneath the city.

Sudden rattling, deli?
A sleepless blue train tunneling
to Jamaica Beach—so many far-brought dins.

Pinching my eyes shut, the refrigerant's
in-heat thrum surges
bruised kiwi, flakes of coconut,

cardamom swamped in syrup. Drones
past the suctionhold to
reverberate this triple-locked rent.

At the shoe-stop, the flag we bannered:
bright red
bridging the green of land to black.

Between them
(& everywhere it seems)
an emphatic white space.

Across Kenya, our still-taken country,
state abductions are flourishing.
Daily. Protesters fished

from roads. A Butcher
jets to DC, smiles to the Oval,
arm stretched for more arms.

To fuck or be fucked?

Across America, state abductions
are flourishing.
A cargo plane fuels to charge

from one tip of the continent
to a heavier fortress
before a gavel bangs—

Across a divided atlas, "Send *them* home"
wrings empires. Across
Palestine, Ukraine, Sudan,

Myanmar, Syria, Haiti,
South China Sea, Baltic Sea, the Atlantic
are sleepers haunting banners of history—

On the other end of the phone,
we turn our faces, unwilling to talk,
some fresh quarrel. You or I

stretch a hand for peace but
stone-hearted armaments ensue.

The winter sun falls
to its knees. We lose & gain
hours.

What pleasures hold
our charged & fluent proximities?

Resident or *alien*,
our colluding teeth,
colliding tongues, the sour oven

of morning
breath, I cross halved oceans

& borrowed cities
to close our flesh to one.

To spoon with or fuck with—what is the difference?

Aperture.   The part

of lips.   Scent of wet clay   a borrowed tongue

strawing
pent-up gasps

or quiet
as night is long,
you or I flesh
the distance to daycome.

I

IN SEARCH OF WA MUTHONI'S GARDEN

It was a small plot and water rarely visited
the pipes even on the Fridays that Nairobi Water had allotted us.
When it did, we flooded drums, jerricans, dishes, plastic cups,
guest-only glasses, spoons. Every firmament is first water.
The plot came last. An unremarkable system.
But the carrots were green then orange, harpooning
the loam, anchoring giant with power, the pumpkins bulbous,
a dense tangle of black nightshade, strength we couldn't dribble past.
It felt almost like stealing—

The ring of passion fruit, a concave spine climbing
into the geoid stone tank like flames over an impenetrable highland,
banana leaves lapping against the house fluid as dry reed
in a basket weaver's hands, the avocado tree, a parable of sunlight,
cool and enduring, limes washing along the bougainvillea fence,
every day exhuming that pungent earth we knew,
how Wa Muthoni's garden so defied the sun,
my god it gave loudly
my god those plums.

ELEGY LATHERED TO ARS POETICA

My mother, a seamstress, wrote
numbers everywhere.

On bales of uncut cloth, mended sleeves,
finished milk packets. The margins

of her King James: *28, 36, 44*—
shoulders, busts dancing across Leviticus,

hips in the spell of David's song.
Her Book of Ruth biroed, circled, bookmarked by an old zipper

like a conceit.
                    Much has faded now.

Those oversize kanga shirts collared with
the shame
                of thinking myself too fashionable, gone—

& something of summer's dusty light
        chews my mind to unprivate rooms,

   that house: sweet peas & ginger, a pinch of salt,
                    the hushed buzz of bills, thankless thoughts,

the rush of her inked arm wheeling
a Singer machine, the flash of a camera.

The Singer's pedal has been vacant
two half-lives now.
Still, looking past—

I see it, finally—
bobbing back & forth

like a finger tongued with spit to clear
a child's teared face

& the needle following through—

ODE TO PLANTAIN

Before your time, you might not believe this, but Ma'Sello ruled the whole village. The songs of praise we sang:

> "Ma'Sello mediates disputes no one can arbitrate
> Ma'Sello receives gifts for fairness, for mercy
> Tributes from many towns over: coral beads, wads of tobacco"

Unfortunately, at night's ripest hour, there was that sister who, staggering from the brewer's den, would curse the whole village nightly. To this day, along that road, the wind remembers things about Ma'Sello that, unfortunately, I cannot mention.

You are young but you must know that insults button the skin like blackjacks. Following you the way a tune carries a song. And, unfortunately, that year of poor harvests, when ten sacks of oranges couldn't be filled, when the last granaries of plantain were emptied, whispers began.

Behind these eyes, I am there now, where, look—the chief's granaries, our granaries of last resort, are being looted. Fattest bulls driven to slaughter. And there—looters are thieving freshwater pots lining the courtyard. Under the plantain stems are the villagers standing guard over Ma'Sello as the embittered crowd mocks her chieftaincy.

I was there. Silent. Ma'Sello's sister stood beside me, chewing an orange or a roasted plantain. My children, we were wrong to stand aside as they uncovered the Royal Stool. Make no mistake. This is no tale of ogres and bellowing ogresses.

Wear your ears. Wear your tongues. Ask the stork to tell the ibis: The grey-crowned crane will sing. O the Royal Stool, how once it stood magnificent as any bank of the Nile!

You might not believe this, but Ma'Sello gave her dethroners into their own hands. What some called *weakness*, others called *forgiveness*. What I know is that one afternoon, the looters' demands, the looters' songs, the looters' drums, the looted Royal Stool—it all began with plantains.

Ma'Sello's chieftaincy brings to mind, the year of thinnest rains, that one season of magpies, our Royal Stool, yes, but mostly plantains.

That is the history of our village, your village. This is why you must sing a dirge to praise a harvest of plantain. And this, my children, is why when you slice open a plantain, it sticks to your fingers.

ODE TO 91.5 RADIO RAHMA

On the Ramadhan Kareem show,
Aziza from Fort Jesus calls to swear she found
the crescent under her thin cushions.

Khadija from Kakuma swears her hidden
red bananas emitted such sickeningly sweet
ethylene, it must have been the crescent.

A voice swallowed by static swears the skies
were clear except for military planes.
Everyone knows the Moon Sighting Committee

is not listening. They will call trusted clerics
for sworn statements. A shopkeeper exits
her kiosk to bark at girls clapping

Baisho I love you, baby, the baby to the sun,
the sun to the owners, the owners to the men . . .
to sing elsewhere. Knobbing the volume,

she finds Radio Rahma paying its bills
with detergent commercials. Five miles
from Shimoni, as his dhow fills with water,

a stranded eel seller sights the crescent.
"Al-Inkishafi," hammered into her ear
at birth, and Siti binti Saad's "Kijiti"

her only flight. Over basalt, a fever of jinis
disperses exhausted from sinking a dhow's
fishing nets. Thirsty for moonlight,

an anglerfish drags a sailor's glass eye
over red coral. A lonely sperm whale
trails a submarine tapping fiberglass cables.

Decompression sickness soon follows.
Elsewhere, inverting a lemon sponge cake,
Waridi wonders whether the gash

of light over the baking tin could be
the neighborhood thief lurking again.
In fiery Arabic littered with Kiswahili,

Bibi Hajja asserts how useless it is
to speculate. The moon's absence is Allah
mercying us with time to mop our hearts.

In any case, fasting is such a gift.
A paper boat sails cold water in a green basin.
A boy pretends to be a fisherman lost

at sea. His father pretends to be the moon.
The boy pretends to be a country.
The moon explodes. A coconut seller's

daughter, who rarely says anything,
spies a girl and two cats lifting off from Mars,
but who will believe a girl who ran from

Koran school? Bi Kidude comets the country
in her soulful "Muhogo wa Jang'ombe."
By now, the dhow is fully submerged.

At a Hilton, the Committee gathers.
Each with his wad of airtime cards.
Soon, they will face Riyadh to rule.

AMBIENT PRISONER'S DILEMMA

We must have seemed so strange
brushing past traders, exorbitant umbrella hawkers,
squeezing through thick processions of secondhand
t-shirts, dresses, corsets held against the body in
that public, most intimate fitting room of the eye's
approximation. Across the stretch, wind thrashed
the dampness of rain.

On we'd go past Ambassadeur, through Accra lane,
sighting the blue-tiled Taj Mahal of bus station
temple. Lining behind the rush hour onslaught
of Community SACCO travellers. Under the fresh
linen of rain, writhing the crooked line's snailpace
before, at last, each of us hoisted ourselves onto
the empty cabin of a matatu.

Everything part of Nairobi's daily horoscope:
worn leather seats, stuck windows, no safety
belts to fasten and no metaphor either.
There was also the driver's late arrival, soaked in
rain's first offertory. Multiple attempts to cough
the cold engine ablaze, its rude awakening.
As though revenge, its heat kettling our seats
as we geared through traffic.

On splashing tarmac, acres of skyscraper shadows,
the piercing appetite of headlights. At the edge
of the city, wide as our whole neighbourhood,
it seemed almost a relief—our tongue-tied selves
hypnotized by the endless grey and green of
the city cemetery—its bedded arrangements:
final, longing still, graceful even.

At accident scenes where traffic again clotted,
our mix of horror, exhilaration, and gratitude
eyeing mangled bodies of vehicles. As though
a misgiving, the chorus of flashing hazard lights,
dissonant hooting—each of us sealed into
our hives of silence, our unpunctuated measures
of fault. Was there anything to say, a night
or two perhaps, before, finally, the parting?
Fruit of impasse, on and on, this bitter tonsil
of regret.

This morning   between us a continent
of cooling time, we both knew it, I now understand,
separately, jointly—our skewered togetherness
unmendable, continuous. None of this, I suppose,
matters much now. Still and all, together
we'd watched those windshield wipers strive
to squeeze each raindrop to nothing.
Each left-right wave parting the mist suddenly
to half the world before us; cloudburst,
its own direction, its own fresh specificities.

Each low roof in the foggy horizon announcing
our nearing to home. Those days, that June,
that cityscape drawing us outside time and time.

II

The pressure of your hand became more tender, more possessive.

—MARIAMA BÂ

ODE TO THE HEAT OF A JUST-VACANT SEAT

I like my ass warm is a terrible way to begin a poem.
I mean it. Thursday night, on the screeching uptown F,
I am in search of an escape. Sometimes, when I'm lonely,
I kiss the inside of my wrist, this way—just so. In *Winter*
Stars, Larry Levis draws a small wind, the size of
a wrist as all that remains between a son and father.
I trust a stranger as much as I mistrust language. Caught
in another's tongue, I—forgive me—the speaking voice,
have been deceitful. I have been rageful.
I'm sad. The best thing about a hug is to allow and be
allowed to find safety in another's heartfelt proximity.
To remind each other, in embrace, how to move toward
the body. There is a poem engraved on a spaceship
headed to Jupiter's icy moon six years and two billion
miles away. Some NASA scientists must think language is
pretty awesome. Sometimes, when I don't know where
I belong, I turn to philosophy, all manner of theories.
Other times, other more honest times, I turn to space
and there! I point to the just-vacant seat, a coat turning
a corner, the stranger whose warmth nests me tonight.

FORM I-589

Today, O dear one, have someone photo you.
Not your passport-size staples or your proofs-of-life

for home. A true life-size in your new country
not watched but seen. Behind you, a bright

red white blue flag brooming summer sun.
Come, practice here at home before the white wall.

Practice how to be framed. A watching lens
is your most unshattered space. Come closer perhaps

to those who may box you in vague description.
Smile. Always smile to whoever captures you.

Be well-seamed on tape. Practice your still life.
Smile to your deadlocked jurors.

Whether or not the subject is already dead
every photograph is this catastrophe.

—ROLAND BARTHES

ODE TO FARMERS' MARKETS

The true American cartels—can I say this?
$15 grade AAAAA keto-friendly nestfresh Eggcellence.

$21 hand-plucked hand-certified cherries. Melt-in-
your-mouth eat-well-sleep-best feast-your-microbes

Jersey kimchi, maple butter barrelled from Montreal.
This is no clever quip, I mean to praise

the crisp very crispy baking Baldwins, unbeatable
$14.92 native Indian corn, the hurry-while-stocks-last

Arab Medjool dates. If there is any critique here, let it be
to the spectacle of myself this early November eyeing

the self-serve grab-&-go $5 cold tea station—please tip,
thank you :) In this land where traders are noiseless,

private as inner rooms, I'm sick for millet porridge &
peanut stew. My yearning cannot be soothed

by the sweet as Fuji blueberry-walnut swirl spelt loaf,
ginger peach jams, the *Vogue*-featured chicken broth.

Among these *Local Flavours, Familiar Faces* sometimes
I feel as looked-at as the vine-to-farm-to-table Merino

scarves, booths of never-late-to-start unsweetened weight-
loss ashwagandha, the improve-your-life Thai succulents.

My longings have longings. Yes, my instinct is to haggle
for the herbicide-free pesticide-free coxcomb, on-sale Togo

African violets but why, two visas later, am I still afraid
to drag America & home through the same sentence?

Once, farmers' markets ago, I saw a trader reach behind
crates of squash for a basket of granadillas,

watched as the bright orange shell cracked to sweet pulp,
black & lush as the char that sweetens poblanos,

sweeter than home before the leaving
but how else is one to know?

FORM I-589

Have I told you yet how at the counters
silence is point-blank?

Alighting the steel drum to the x-ray
machine's oversight. On the other side

of the agent's stamp, all your sooths—
the cement of millet flour, winter hibiscus,

black tea, makhana, Royco—
though dried & clear-sealed,

everything you need-have-done
is unzipped, swabbed, re-probed,

crumpled as the work of a fist.
Your *randomized* riffle. Your blue glove.

Your horde of papers, a perfect myth
to stow with your homecrumbs.

COOKING GAS COMMERCIAL

The boy sprinting from Wa Mso's Shopping Center with a transparent polythene bag half-full of kerosene at sunset—past Big Spot Barber Shop, Think Twice Secondhand Clothes, through a rain of sparks from Samson's Weldings before disappearing between Johnnie Walker's Keep Walking Pub and God's Favourite Wines and Spirits—where is he flying to?

FORM I-589

Whatever you ask of me, Love, whatever you say
I am bound by forms to make yours.

You're so gorgeous, so multicultural
America, where are *you* from?

Oh no, no, no—What I meant was,
where are you *originally* from?

You're so well-spoken, Honey,
where did you learn such free speech?

Your liberties, a dazzling commonwealth,
aren't you *mixed* with something?

What & who lands you here?
What & who holsters your where-from forms?

Beginning to endstop, whatever you say,
America, I am bound by this form to refrain.

ARS FINIS

A son fetches his father's thirst-quencher from the shops.
A 1-litre bottle of Koko Kora, chilled, always chilled.

Or glassing your Koko Kora warm for you to know where things stood
between us—I, seared by your urgent gods—work elsewhere.

Even then, I would rush to peel plastic from the undersides of Koko Kora
bottle tops, keying your Motorola Timeport with the hidden code. A chance

to win an all-expenses-paid trip to Seychelles, Mauritius was it? None of us
had passports, had eyed the bounty of neighboring provinces.

—

I, who was not allowed sugar, on other days, Hosanna, would be given Daima yogurt.
Now the opulence of pineapple, caramel-flavoured yogurts mist the perishing shelves.
Aisles of diet and zero-sugar Koko Koras superabundant as energy drinks.

—

Yesterday, years after kiting the valley for the North—a small fluorescent room,
rows of wine bottle corks, balconied against a leafless window (call it habit or

sincere imitation)—I caught your voice, a glottal shimmer in my chest:
"To whittle the sweetest cane, Morio, dance, dance with red ants."

Your sunfall adage obsidian as your cool glass of Koko Kora, facing the orange
roads, impermanent tributaries long gone, the ambulatory Eastbound taxis,
an emptied bottle dewing your dark three-legged stool.

Yesterday, reaching as soothsay, I longed to uncap, savour each drop of Daima.
Longed to polish my index finger over the arena of the yogurt tin, wend

my tongue over the aluminum lid—saccharine shelf-life extender,
euphonious keeper of dark and air, girding delight past the last dot!

—

Now, as though by some great refrangible light, we have bartered places.

You recite the same tales over and over (some happened, other outright fictions)
before scooping yourself woodenly into the cluttered house.

Buried under your turned-up radio news bulletin, the receiver sails on . . .
and on . . . under the Atlantic as I brim an iron-walled world.

Now, I know better than to angle faded negatives against the light. To peel vial after vial
from perishing shelves. To kite after a liquidized embrace.

Now, as though by the light of a match, my limbs longer, hairline skinning
to fettle a V, furrows netting my bewilderment, I crunch the prized

chicken neck between swigs of Sprite, save its crusty skin for last.
A toothpick corners my mouth, a promissory *home soon*, a too-late sms.

Now, it appears, I am almost a father. Almost your son.

FORM I-589

After his election, President-elect Lincoln traveled from Springfield to DC, undocumented and disguised through secret routes to prevent assassination attempts.

Here my children have been born . . . I now leave, not
knowing when, or whether ever, I may return . . .

You, wanting, wanted, and unwanted by the union . . .
Ellipses are a song for your lawful self . . .

Ellipses thread the mystic chord of memory . . .
Ellipses suture the leaving and the uncertain journey . . .

Ellipses are safe trails across treacherous borders . . .
Ellipses declare you will live, survive, thrive . . .

O dear one, you crossing the states 200 miles & more . . .
You whose inaugural oath is colluded against . . .

Ellipses are concealment . . . A form of asylum
precedent as these states . . .

who can go with me, and remain
with you, and be everywhere for good . . .

ELEGY

Is there a response to goodbye

ODE TO DOSA MAN

Washington Square Park South

03/01	Thirikumar "Dosa Man" Kandasamy	– $8	masala dosa	🔒
03/03	Qahwah House	– $7.45	latte	🔒
03/04	James Clinton	– $1450	FEBRUARY	Pending
03/05	H.	+ $100	crossing ½ of china ✈️🌏	🔒
03/06	James Clinton	– $1450	FEBRUARY	🔒
03/08	H.	– $100	🔙	🔒
03/08	Thirikumar "Dosa Man" Kandasamy	– $9	pondicherry dosa	🔒
03/11	chuffed.org	– $20	Mahmoud Khalil	Pending
03/11	Thirikumar "Dosa Man" Kandasamy	– $70	15 samosa with sambar + tip	🔒
03/12	A. K.	+ $9	iftar :)	🔒
03/13	Pumho	+ $9	only feets 😥	Pending
03/20	V.	– $23	no other land 🎥🎬	🔒
03/22	Thirikumar "Dosa Man" Kandasamy	– $11	veggie uttapam w coconut chutney	🔒
03/23	James Clinton	– $1500	MARCH + its late fee	🔒
03/25	Erin	– $54.35	Jan + Feb elec gas (47.08 + 61.62)	🔒
03/28	chuffed.org	– $10	Rümeysa Öztürk	Pending
03/28	Thirikumar "Dosa Man" Kandasamy	– $9	masala dosa, spicy, green sauce :)	🔒

FORM I-589

You, who were and are dying
to arrive again.

You, who cannot afford not to watch
the price-alerts, the news.

You, whose presence stands
between a great country & greatness.

You, whose absence maddens
a great country.

Such power. O dear one,
whoever claims to be greatened in

your abscence, affirms
in the same breath, your power.

when they come for us/ I build safety
inside you/ & wake in cuffs

—FATIMAH ASGHAR

ODE TO INCEST DISGUISED AS LITANY

In Aisha's hadith, Allah, who has no need to be wise or careful,
is gentle, loves gentleness, rewards it more than any other.

Moments ago, you promised that if I quarreled you, tears
would come. Reading the frown lines above your glasses,
I fetched from the bag of bags a place for the groceries.

On either side of our fromfroms, there are numerous tongues.
In this one, *beloved* is sweetless. It is in "ibn am" where pleasure
resides. An idiom that translates, you reveal, to *the son of my uncle.*

Ninety-nine names for love, mercy, the beauty of Allah is
Allah can be called into any room.

At Kroger, standing before the self-checkout counters,
again I lose restraint—accept my faults: orange-rind
chocolate, custard apples, a net of pluots which please

you to explain are grafts of plums and apricots.
We are not cousins. You insist I make this clear for the reader.

Sometimes, pressing grains of rice to your tongue,
folding clumps of flour sinkside, at the stove lighting
coals for oud, I—the beloved's admittedly unfunny voice—

mock the Arabic, the wise ancients, their delicious
idioms, your other ibn ams, a faultless net of pluots,
that I—the beloved's serious voice—cherish.

Forgive me. Habibty, such water.

FORM I-589

Whatever others may say, each of us carries
a flag in their heart, some unwilting occupancy.

Listen. You, who is alert to too many flags
in these states, knowing too well the shrapnel

of allegiance to too many lands.
You, watching with trepidation

as greatening the states greatens the prison-
industrial complex, the cargo hold manifests.

Listen. Your inimitable name is itself sanctuary.
Even the claim that your absence greatens

the nation betrays and codifies your sovereignty.
Inside each of us is a truer validity.

A shared world where prayer
is the only form, only petition.

III

The hawk plays with the pigeon and the pigeon is happy, but not knowing that it is playing with death.

—AMOS TUTUOLA

THE TAPSTERS

When the Academy of Sommeliers sought to bolster their meagre cellars, they called on the Land of Tapsters. Thanking the tapsters for their hospitality, the red-wine sommelier rose and spoke as though a bowl of water sat in his mouth.

An apprentice tapster rose from the crowd, "Idiot of Idiots, I welcome you." The sommeliers smiled the joyless smile of biting hard bread. "Palm wine is fruit of the gods, a whisk of sense and the senseless." That was the first lesson.

The next evening, under a great cashew tree, a tapster with the looseness of a throat familiar with songs broke the air. "Palm wine is the deliciousness of yams sizzled with basil and seasoning cubes. With ancestors, prophecies from the gods, and palm wine, we are fortified."

From her mouth, red butterflies flew to the anthill, bent themselves into the shape of a chair as was custom. When a great wind rearranged the air, a pot of great age and ornate patterns sat in the chair's place. "At the next moon, carry your tongues for palm wine."

As the undernourished sommeliers retreated, the tapsters danced the dance of eyes among which a secret thrived.

The next moon, the white-wine sommelier shouldered their gadgets: a glass decanter, the sucking sound of front teeth, golden spitting techniques.

"Palm wine is the red red red of a rooster soaked in heated mustard oil," a tapster sang. A string of saliva was seen wetting sweet-wine sommelier's mouth. "Palm wine never sleeps! It is a wrapper opened and closed with haste to redden the firewood!" The tapsters roared.

"Palm wine," a drunkard from the crowd joined, "is a cup of fleas. Swifter than a plaiter's hand, a leopard's shadow." An avalanche of cashews fell, shattering the decanter. A line of ants entered the gathering to claw each glass piece away.

From the anthill, a swarm of orange butterflies seethed. Each vomited a half kilo of palm wine into the pot.

"Oshun is harvests," a senior tapster began. "Agwu is health. Obatala! We seek the heads of our enemies in this great calabash." The fruit-heavy cashew swung fiercely West, North, East, South.

Though no one could confirm it, a tapster claimed to have spotted a nine-legged spider on the cashew, so libation was poured to thunderous claps. "The banjo has swallowed the flute," a senior tapster conceded at last. Everything sat in its place.

Restless as fruit flies, the sommeliers approached the pot. The eldest tapster dipped the cup of honour, poured libation, then held it out to the sommeliers.

The sommeliers began to speak in the deliciousness of idioms and proverbs, each clueless tongue tantalized by palm wine. Tapsters danced the dance of sense and senseless with the sommeliers until red weaverbirds gonged the air.

Upon returning to the Academy, occupation plans were drawn.

CONTRASUTURE

First time English is in your mouth, you burn
with the smell of illicit brew, chopped kale and
three overripe tomatoes in a polythene bag
between your left rib and patched elbows.

Hours after English takes you, word arrives of
municipal bulldozers lined to hole our beaten rooms.
Camouflaged officers, their wet loot of blood-red paint
marking houses for demolition, room for police posts.

Your arthritic hands swollen just as well from
twisting a stable mattress-and-furniture origami
ligatured by your strict leather waist-braid, hauled into
cheap flight of air by your hard school of obedience.

And a while later, I watched you, flickering beneath
a bent streetlamp, my leaver already, throttling past
the cratered kiosks, murmurous in the womb
of a reeking overcoat, onward to the bus station plaza.

The year of Englishes was the year of wet charcoal.
Cold cassava lidded with rainwater boiled to
fudge sweet as the sweep of found Milo packets,
prices quartered, notch after singed tear-notch.

What I prize of Englishes is the lick of tang-soured
count. Peals of laughter syllabled over the whir
of lost smokes. Teaching the townspeople improper,
illegible hide-and-seek from a flanked escort.

What I recollect of your, my Englishes
is the rote of your crackling baritone
hung in air so buried, so urgent, so alive
but never in excess—

BEFORE THE CLIMATE CLOCK

This morning, I remembered the watch repairer on Wangari Maathai Road
who sits under an upturned soda crate. Just past the jacaranda's stump
where geckos used to sun themselves.

Now across the street from there, where Lotto kiosks and Instant Logbook Loans
are sprouting. Watch out for tuk tuks zipping past, the dark pools from Shell
and OiLibya filling stations. If still lost, greet a stranger, and open your ears.

The watch repairer with her numerous faces. Tweezing and wheeling
each fogged, flooded, fire-ravaged sphere. Watch her hand removers
hacking seconds.

Bob Marley's "War" wails from her mediumwave at the top of each hour
as Giddi na Ghost sellotape comewestays across the country on live. Her laughters,
nods of puzzlement as her movement holders mend pasts and half-pasts.

Sundays too. In the crush of florals, black, and purple as at a deacon's funeral.
Her weathered sisal apron setting escapements.

O Repairer, shake my hand if you will. I greet you tomorrow from this side
of the world inside the rooster's wail.

THE CURE

Seven years. Vigilance. But today, packing Ghana Must Go bags, a fatigue so instant, so top-volume gonged me.

Do you guess? I love you, Tuku.

I watch you squeeze that last dollop of margarine from the packet, look over our sparse furniture, yellowed walls. "I feel it again. Everywhere. The evil eye—I am found. Anywhere else. We move. We must."

So many provinces stand between this town and your Old Village. Our lives here are far from those goldmines flooded with bats, the shrines of witch doctors you believe to dim your dreams.

I love you as you wake from tossing sleeps of sweat with visions. Lean over the balcony. Fixate on moths drawn translucent by the security light—another omen, such fires.

Three towns ago, I visited a witch doctor. The cure, he'd said, "Two white guinea fowls. Throats sliced. Unlaid yolks plucked. Kneaded to bitter bread. Three garlics. Buried in a shallow grave."

Years of leavings. Here, at last, we have a town. I'm scared. And knowing it is the bus which comes only tomorrow that holds us here this night—

Have I made riddles of my love? Its lengths? From the beans, I winnow out pintos, yellow and black eyes. I part and knead yolkless doughs. I gouge eyes sprouting from potatoes.

Four towns. Four market towns of the amulet around your neck. Four good-neighboured towns of lifting the house to sweep for the evil eye.

From the table where I sit to lick this envelope, I hear the doctor's grave instruction. I lace my boots. I knob the door—accuse me of wanting so much the door.

I sheaf the dark with a pressure lamp. Peel the pepper tree's soil. Retract its roots. I plant your cure. Irrigate the grave. I staple the loam with pebbles. A slice of moon, a lightward sigh. This odor of feathers. A fist of peppers. A teethy kiss leaned into your ear.

Such silent sleep now. Siloed away in dreams. For once.

Won't you come awake?

Why won't you come awake?

THE COFFIN MAKER

The Book of Dreams I inherited is septic.
My dead linger in the thresholds.

I am the traffic officer's hand; such severe
gesticulation. There! I point to a small wind,

the stream cut to cool the millstone.
I am washed out and emptied,

emptied and washed out, I am rice.
At its most centrifugal, grief floors me

to praise my dead. Spirits howl and bray
my incus. The eye at the back of my head

is widowed by leukemia, breast cancer,
and wild fowls. I am soft, malleable.

The most eager burial firmament.
I am pine. No more the rotted hands

creasing my shirts. I slice and slice and slice
the boards. Six brass handles,

three kilos of plastic wreath, nine tonnes
of ochre, each joinery will hold

what the spirit world cannot bear.
I will climb the grave absolutely alone.

I am the heap and heft, the thump and vault
of earth. I am the taste of metal in your lungs.

I am blisters wetting your feverish hands.
Dawn, each varnished box will be shouldered.

Maggots will bore the dead to hush.
I will be light as I was at birth.

ELEGY LOTIONED INTO ARS POETICA

I had to try to describe that particular condition which was—is—the living proof of my inheritance. And, at the same time, with that very same description, I had to claim my birthright.

—JAMES BALDWIN

Nights, I'd ruminate on your sour well of riddles
as though you had avowed never to say it plain, the anecdotes

tipping you at each turn to new conversation   Nights
woken again by your snoring, I'd tiptoe to your room

half-irrigated by candlelight, find you defeated,
murmuring in your work clothes   Nearer I'd draw

to your goings in & out of coherence, whole minutes of
the broken Englishes you speak in Kiswahili & Gĩkũyũ

dreamlands unlettered as hearsay in the day-end
creases of your cream-coloured shirt   Morning,

at the district school, the son sketches as a teacher
of English chalks tasteless covenants of grammar & soon

the older son, at a loss for words—his weaverbird
diseasing, gone—will excavate from spadefuls of memory

the wonted telling—a void bittersweet
as a language called to question   To speak

in our Englishes is to clamour to lay inside your voice,
to canal into the Babel of my ear your breath

I who carries your line draw your near-whisper—*come*
across—sear, soothe, soar, echo, boom my vow,

my wells, my names, my dear dear consonance
you, against the dying light, my windbox, are the gate

through which every language that has sought to swallow
ours will tiptoe wordless around

You're my imperfect citizenship, truer song I sing,
my lyric, my syntax, my diction, my armaments

Kadoom. / Kadoom. Kadoom. Ka- / doooom. Kadoom. Now
I have beaten a song back into you, / rise & walk away like a panther.

—YUSEF KOMUNYAKAA

IV

. . . the priest and the doctor
In their long coats
Running over the fields.

—PHILIP LARKIN

NOMENCLATURE

Can't she hear? Tell her.
Tell her a tenant is knocking
the president's face against the window.

Tell her to fetch the book of borrowings.
That president's face is not enough
to buy milk.

—

When debts are tidal, a tenant learns
to fetch through the child: Coca-Cola,
geometry set, British Embassies.

Mercy, the loan officer scolds,
is not a friend of debt. To crawl
from credit to debit, axe your hand.

—

Two crates of Broadways, five fists
of garlic, magadi salt are lean stock
to ward off the auctioneer's din.

NOW LETTING. CALL TO RENT
A sign tall as the child is moosed
around the lock. Who wouldn't

learn to minus from shame?
Where to source two packets
of 500 ml Daima for the shoes

outside the single room? Deacons
reciting the tentmaker's letters
to Corinth clouded

by the steam of mung beans.
She manages past
their bowed heads.

SEMIOTICS

TIRED OF DEBT?
TIRED OF IN-LAW?
TIRED OF LAND GRABBERS?
TIRED OF SMALL TITHE?
TIRED OF DEATH?
TIRED OF INTERNET SHUTDOWN?
TIRED OF BAD ROADS?
TIRED OF CANCER?
TIRED OF WAITING FOR BENEFITS?
TIRED OF VISA REJECTIONS?
TIRED OF BAD BBL?
TIRED OF MAN UNITED LOSING?
FIRST CONSULT FREE.
WITCH DOCTOR FOR HIRE.

THE DOOR

That's what I remember.
My mind trawling sunrise & sunset,

lashing wind & the coming of angels.
Whole damn years composed of

the shame that walled me from home.
In my motherland, I was Locust fruit.

The guest who chores a host to watered-down beans.
In my fatherland, I was

the diet of too-many-guavas knotting the intestines.
Dazed by griefs, I left home.

Years of borrowed beds, deep cups of liquors
to unbrood, I was

the red rooster urgent for a scrim of light
& the nightlong reward

was all my shades of weakness & failures.
In those wounded years,

I carried everything myself.
Believed it was the only road.

Fanning the fume, I cannot help
but remember Okonkwo

whose buried griefrage
twice emptied his seat in Umuofia

to a foreignhomeland.
The breeze has blown.

I have yawned away my years dressed in rage
like a mother waiting at the door in the evening

for a child, a blue slipper in hand, her rage tremulous as joy
upon seeing her child's turn

of a corner—the long road, acres of bathing stars, barking shadows.
I mean to look through the years

I believed myself debtless to this world.
It was the year of the Mask. Healers took to lecterns like

fuming Oracles. Heads of the pouring dead.
It was the year of the Mask &

Friends, I wanted to die.
What I remember most of those days is exhaustion

in laughter. How often my face fell.
That &

how the purple grillegates of Holy Redeemer Gospel Church across the street
from that last borrowed room

at the edge of town
opened

each Sunday at six
to those deserted streets, without so much

as a creak. Opened
like a half-step,

sorrow managed to a soft sob
& only just. Still here,

all I have to do is open the door.
Death will wait. Believe me, O dear one.

All, all you have to do is
open the door.

ARTIST STATEMENT

The barber testing the bite
of her clippers on her powdered palm,
doesn't she know electricity is out?

ODE TO MANGO LUBE

The man standing inside Trust Me Kemist Ltd waits
for everyone else to buy—paracetamols, hydrochlorothiazides,
Brufens, a glucometer—before sliding a crumpled note
to the pharmacist. Not just the teeth marks on his neck—
all that way, all that dust, all that patience, you can tell.

—

"Riddle Riddle!"
        "Riddle come!"

"Riddle Riddle!"
        "Riddle come! Riddle come!"

"The sweet eaters came with something to eat.
 Out of the eating came something sweet.
 Out of the eaten came something sweeter."

STILL LIFE, NATIONAL HOSPITAL

The gurney rattling
the corridor at 2:13 a.m.
is Suleiman.

The longest detainee
at National
Teaching Hospital.

3 years of a pending bill,
arms broken,
(drunken taxi, run).

Suleiman presses
his thumb against necks
(pulsing or cold).

Shuts
(the scrim of)
glassy eyes,

(to aid
night nurses).
Gurneys the dead.

Pries
the hazardous waste elevator.
(to postmortem lien).

—

Another shortage
of nurses
(even the hour passes),

no attempt to resuscitate
the still-warm
(in public wards).

Air not-yet-sharpened
by wailings
(of visitor hours).

—

Suleiman
(no insurance
poor harambee)

is who
the new nightstaff,
desperate with questions,

find:
backup generator,
the maze of

chemo-only toilets,
systemdown Social Health,
filing expedited requests

to press food from,
wash your dead
(untrained).

—

Forks of tomato rice,
a lunch pawpaw
left

to Suleiman
(by the Director)
to learn

who's stealing
hours,
who's openhanded

with antibiotics
(little wounds).
A chance, soft

as vaseline,
to trim (for both)
the fat of debt.

To near
the taxi drivers
(asleep, faces

squeezed at last
in hats),
the neem trees

trembling
(faintly)
outside Casualty.

ENDLESS TRAFFIC

The fantastic thing about South Africa is one always and only meets one's friends through politics.
—BESSIE HEAD

At a roundabout, a woman greets the woman seated next to her in the matatu. After roads, they lower their voices to enter maize prices, Parliament's capture, reckless politicians, unsolved femicides.

TRIGGER WARNING

At Eulogy Services Cyber Cafe, a woman in camouflage is laminating

POLICE IS YOUR FRIEND
POLICE IS YOUR FRIEND
POLICE IS YOUR FRIEND
POLICE IS YOUR FRIEND
POLICE IS YOUR FRIEND
POLICE IS YOUR FRIEND
POLICE IS YOUR FRIEND
POLICE IS YOUR FRIEND
POLICE IS YOUR FRIEND
POLICE IS YOUR FRIEND
POLICE IS YOUR FRIEND
POLICE IS YOUR FRIEND
POLICE IS YOUR FRIEND
POLICE IS YOUR FRIEND

THE WAKE

Wa Vini is dunking stained tea cups in soap water. Behind her,
a yellow shirt pegged under a red shirt hangs on the rusted wire line.
The southeasterlies disturb a fence of fever trees.

Someone is opening the mabati gate to fetch bread at Wa Njoro's Blessings shop.
Away from seeing eyes, at the corner of the road, a great sobbing releases.

Mama Otieno rushes from the kitchen, where a pot of boiled milk is plucked
from the fireplace, returned and plucked, till the nutmeg and black pepper bloom.

On the veranda, a neighbour is pressing the widow's Nokia between her left ear
and shoulder where it tugs her faux pearl earring. Watch her punch the son's
Casio: 2610 a sack of basmati, 3976 pishori.

A locksmith is heaving a crowbar against the wardrobe's doors, whose keys only
he knew. Time to dust deeds, British American Insurance receipts.

A crate of Broadways enters the gate. A well of misery over Mrs. Wahome's eyes.
First, it was her. Mr. Wahome long gone, a plot of napier grass over him near
the compost. And now her friend.

The women have managed, at last, to convince Mrs. Njogu to chew.
A spoon of salted avocado. One more. Last one. No. Enough.

The 5-month-old in Mrs. Njogu's right hand is shrieking so Mrs. Njogu is lifting
her blouse, cupping her breast, waving it in the air, her cracked nipple finding
the baby's hair, nose, eyes, and finally mouth.

A firefinch warbles off.

An aunt is fishing the bereaved daughter's schoolbag for a ruler and a Home Science
exercise book. She draws columns and rows page after page. Date, name, harambee amount.
Now there is a condolence book.

A queue worries past.

Someone refreshes a glass pitcher with rainwater.

Under the Men's Fellowship tent, a man is digging his pockets for a handkerchief.
Someone will grab the mic from Treasurer Ananias to baritone "Mwathani Wakwa
Njakaniria Tawa."

Children are laughtering all over, playing Police and Robber around a red Corolla.

Behind a latrine door that will not lock, a boy coats a slug in coarse salt.

Mabrigan has sat beside the bereaved son to sketch his father's face
breathed into with life. By now, formaldehyde has disorganized his face.

At the corner of the tent, a cluster of maroon suits discusses where to tailor
a new Men's Fellowship suit. Boxers or briefs?

Who and when to meet at God Gives God Takes Final Rites Home?
Who to lift, carry, dress Mr. Njogu?

Mrs. Ibrahim, who studies cannabis strains at the National Research Institute,
is washing her hands for a second and third time before chopping the spinach.

> "Malaika nakupenda Malaika
> Malaika ningekuoa Malaika
> Malaika nakupenda Malaika"

The song in the window is Mrs. Njogu, who must shawl baby Born Living
over her back, must rock and lull, rock and lull before laying him on the mattress
where he will wail and wail to crawl the cold floor.

The shifting lamplight shadow is Deacon Sapphira pacing. They are trying to find
a PA system. A wedding has rented church speakers, the small Sunday School
YAMAHA, the pastor.

So. Who will minister Kohelethu? Who will have the first last look?

Mrs. Wahome is shouting at the women near the garden. Someone must follow Mrs. Njogu, who, needing to be useful, is carrying a sharp knife and a basin into the garden. Mr. Njogu's last spring onions.

After agreeing how to split the metal plate heaped with boiled chickpeas,
a shirtless gravedigger floats a laddering arm into the rim.

At the compost, a thread of ants skitter over mango peels and a heap
of ruinous sketches.

In one, Mabrigan has charcoaled a tiny birthmark below Njogu Jr.'s earlobe
where, years from now, between sheets brined with pleasure, a paid-for lover
will rag his haphazard tongue.

By now, the condolence book is wrinkled with psalms.
"Jesus, Jesus, how I love Thee" is quieting.

The agrovet has volunteered to call in to Mũũga FM at 8 p.m., obit hour.

A local sports commentator will MC on Friday. But only after 2.
(AFC is playing Sofapaka at 11). Which is fine.

THE SWEET KEEPERS

Stern as an errand, they summon
their grandchildren from playing kalongolongo.

He stretches his trembling hands
above a stone wardrobe.

Past yellowed pension promissories, birth and death papers,
is a cool blackcurrant juicebox.

She reaches underneath the mattress
for a pouch with banded letters, a plastic rose,

a baby's left shoes,
and the sweetness of the sweetest sweets

around. This elderly,
skin-sweet pair.

Each with their keeping place
keeping on.

V

Ah done been tuh de horizon and back and now
Ah kin set heah in mah house and love by comparisons
Dis house ain't so absent of things . . .

—ZORA NEALE HURSTON

ODE TO THE INVITING COLDNESS OF A PILLOW

I work my palms to fluff the cushion until my face feathers the surface like a sketch on tracing paper.

Tonight, I will stroll right into sleep, meet the shock of darkness, the beauty of God, judgment.

—

Twice, I have begged for love.

Afraid I'd need to be loved again. Afraid I'd need to move again. I bedded myself in septic dreams.

—

In silent films, to draw the teeth and slapped thighs of laughter, the actor runs across the stage hysterically. Some journeys, of course, mean more than others.

—

Sometimes, facing the ceiling's harsh sterility, I crave motion but the image in my head that I masturbate to is slow to recover.

—

Other times, the veined back of my tongue rushes the steep hall of my mouth.

Two unround patches of sweat soaking the sheets. Three or four pumps of soap.

—

Sometimes, the heated bursts of flow oscillating from the fan seem too determined to deodorize the smell of my sex.

At twenty-five feet per second, the supercharged motor wafts its excess before burying itself in Sleep mode.

Only so much night is left now.

—

Sometimes the smell of my sex is so lone, so easily eclipsed, I am left low again, folding my hand again, reaching again.

Other times, I'm so finished, I crash to sleep before the gasp and cold pressure of a pulled-open wet wipe.

God, I do not praise myself enough, but what more have I to master in the art of raking run-off across my belly? My beating heart, my thighs, hairy, I so love.

—

My body is a house I entered without knocking.

America enters without knocking.

—

I promised my visa I would not to say shit about America.

Baldwin said that to love America is to insist on criticizing her perpetually.

Some day, I will love you Migwi, but right now I am trying to engrave you into this loam.

—

In 1765, as a student of law, Thomas Jefferson bought a translated copy
of the Holy Quran to chart a discourse of white freedoms in Virginia & later,
freedoms for any "infidel of any denomination."

Everywhere I don't look, there is precedent for sentimentality.

—

I am trying to face you, O dear one. I am trying to face you more naked.

To reach you without elegy—

—

To turn pain to joy, some ancient texts prescribe purging desire. There is song, prayer, prophecy, and more suffering.

The most moving prayer I know is Nina Simone's "Mississippi Goddamn."

—

More than we would like to admit, a nation-state's survival is dependent upon its enemies even & especially if the enemy is the nation-state itself.

—

More than we would like to admit, the easiest recipe for war is individuals asserting their freedoms inside a border.

—

Somewhere between yesterday & home, I will love, absolutely, this faulty container of you, Migwi.

—

My best example of how we might survive or thrive is Mohammed Ali's footwork.

More than we would like to admit, the other alternative is often footwork.

—

More than we would like to admit, poverty, miseducation, and hate are robust pipelines for a nation's survival.

—

There are days I almost want to say thank you, Migwi, for the heat trickling down your razor-burned sex. Evenings when I hunger to pumice your feet, lotion your thighs, excite your dandruff, clip your nails, coat your roots with castor oil.

Nights when I reach and reach—

> *in one such case a woman was found so forcefully fornicating with her feet the soil under her that they thought she was attempting to bury her own body while standing upright. When pressed, she confessed that she had heard of travel and was attempting to push her body through to the other side of the world*
>
> *—there are many such cases*

—DIVYA VICTOR

CONSULAR STILL LIFE

The woman fetching a yellow slip from
the metal basin at American Embassy
counter six—come. Let us leave
the sorrow folding your face here.

ALL THE WAY FROM THERE TO HERE

Folding notes around her middle finger,
twice counting coins for change,

a bus conductor with a black face mask
pulled over her chin says

"Asante Auntie, Asante, Asante sana,"
to each passenger alighting

herehere, herethere, therenothere
onto murram roads, past barbed keiapple

MARKED MBWA KALI USIKOJOE HAPA,
onward to brown zinc roofs,

night thickblue as thieves.
Across the town, the hum of crinkled khaki,

felled cushions, a knifed envelope,
quieted lips, stretched radio antennas.

The scent of a hung wig, a struck match,
unscented baby powder,

kerosene and boiled beans
steaming lighted windows.

THE ATTENDANT

One foot planted
on the cypress bedframe,
he squeezes a blue bottle

of solidified coconut oil,
thin white threads
liquifying between his palms.

He oils the cracks
of his feet, and the fungalskin
between his toes.

He carries his stomach,
trapping with oil
slips of water between

the folds. Mind
elsewhere,
he oils his pubic hair,

down to where
a soldier, British,
squeezed

a pair of pliers.
Only a stump
left.

A clock's pendulum
sweeps the hour.
He scarfs

the scabs on his neck
where, in
a detention camp,

an askari whipped
the memory
of his land, stolen

for settlers, almost—
and his whole body
froths with violent

laughter. From his scalp,
oil rivers into
his dull right ear.

He swirls his wrist
on a cotton swab,
nearly losing balance.

Plumbed
from mind to stomach,
an ache for sweetness

salivates his jaws.
He dabs two drops
of coconut oil

on a finger, opens
his mouth dentist-wide.
Five teeth left.

Separate.
The rest caked in dust
in a storage box

labelled "Mau Mau Rebellion"
in the vault
of a National Museum.

He straightens his back,
a litre of blood
sinks to his feet.

A green housefly
rubs its hands
numinously, but

it is two moons early.
A headless scarecrow
gasps

in the gust of
countless palms.
A Telecom tower hawks

its red searchlight
over tea plantations,
the maximum security

prison, the army base
where British soldiers
are training

for wars. Over carrion
combed by ploughs.
Sprouting

purple vines.
Thousands of eyes stirring
beneath the loam.

PRAYER

Wake by first light to the sound of you scrubbing
  sleep from your face, a tin of fetched rainwater,
the rest fed to hibiscus bushes behind the house.

Under the yeast of morning sun, we trek
  to the fields where we'll pluck okra,
pull fruit against stem after white-flowered stem,

haggle with a vulture of brokers. From the far end,
  the percussion of plastic crates stacked full
of fresh vibrant okra. We watch brokers crew them

  into pick-up trucks for market. Again,
the weary crescendo: a tide of aches. Let it be
  the sudden flood of fruitless stalks.

By now, afternoon. Pocket-heavy, we soak
  the sun's glare. Eye neighbouring fields.
Measure ours against those, scale their extents

of aphids, witchweeds. Leafiest plots memorized
  for inquiries after. Home, in low tongues,
we recount the more daring, most vexing brokers.

Their new formulas of guilt: impunctualities.
   Scribbles of total kilograms, colder soil,
largest okra retrieved. We mark from catalogues

the season's best seeds, corresponding numbers
   of manure wheelbarrows, cross off the lather
of low-yield brands. The respite of equatorial

summers easing our quiet, private lives.
   Half, full moons up and down the ridge.
Against this side of the tin roof, hail

or jinns? Let it be long rains season.
   Let it be rest, boredom,
 tending to what again lands us here.

NIGHT BEFORE THE WEDDING

When visiting hours for the bridal party have passed,
the widow daring to marry again reaches underneath
her bed. Her hand, a bouquet of almond henna,
retrieves a box that once held her lover's ear.
She opens the door. She opens the door only after
knocking is heard. A sigh opens the door.
As quietly as she can, she opens the door without
looking. The door opens the hand tightened around
her throat. She opens the door like the first evening
her great-grandmother sobbed. The door opens
like dissolved paracetamol washed down. She opens
the door like a silver band slid from a finger.
The door opens aware that it is a door. She opens
the door like morning in a different bed.
The door opens its refusal. She opens the door
with a pleading touch. Shame opens the door.
She opens the door like a woman alone in the dark
opening a door. An in-law claiming property opens
the door. She opens the door like a box within a box.
The door cracks open to let just a little light.
She steels herself to open the door. The door wasps
open. Like notes of citrus under an orange tree,
she unzips the door. The door opens a retraction.
She opens the door like a follicle of closure.
Who is left to tell her not to weep into her orange sari?

ODE TO KANDA BONGO MAN'S "MY LOVE ELISABETH"

I have begun to wear my life as a widower.
What came came. Finally, Dede, I will roll
my sleeves to grief. The book of days says

January but the clock's hands stand attention.
I aside the curtains. The mason paning
a broken window left his fingers everywhere.

Behind the prints are see-through shadows,
small images of myself everywhere. I'm
exhausted. Daily, my list of fixings grows:

wobbly chairs, eucalyptus tall as to sag
the power line, a gaping hole in the fence.
Let me shade your grave longer, Dede.

The hammering on the roof?
It is short rains drowning the maize.
A plate of pilau njeri warms the table.

Wole, my across-the-fence friend, is behind
the clock. A week ago, I batteried the radio.
Again it is graining like static between stations.

All week, the mason's whistle has seeded
an earworm. This worn sleeveless cassette
is Kanda Bongo Man tickling my ear:

"Born Living, you must play me."
I obey. The reward is "My Love Elisabeth"
vomited from the speakers' honeycomb mouth

some people de want ask me for you, my love
i say but why you go come back many years

The hour of street lights.

A lighted veranda, wet piles of lumber,
that copse of pear trees. Kanda Bongo Man
is still playing though now he is the sweetlessness

of too much truth, a story without corners.
    I bought air ticket for you to go to London . . .
    I hear that now, you are in New York . . .

    That neighbour who was with you . . .
    I come a drunkard . . .
    Now Johnnie Walker walking on my head

"If Kanda Bongo Man doesn't make you dance o,
call ambulance," Dede would say, "you're dead."
Dede's dying is not yesterday or last year.

I wine my stomach, count our lives: five sons,
thirteen grandsons, the one great-granddaughter
who wears Dede's name beyond us.

Sometimes, shaken by an orchestra of ululations
from that fence, there—next to Wole's
compound—I talk to myself with Dede.

How right she was: there is no assurance
like the visitation of daughters, but why repeat
what you know to its full stops, Dede?

See that black hen? The fat one, the reddest comb
beaking the grass. No. That one there quarreled
by the rest? After scattering grains, I would rush

to separate it from others, it's just that now
I manage only heres-and-theres, theres-and-
heres. Sometimes, on the veranda step,

twisting the suede tin, polishing my BATA shoes
to an inch of their life, the hens remind me
of the fresh Ndombolo the young ones

are dancing now. Ours has been relegated
to Zilizopendwa. Kanda Bongo Man
is sugaringsugaring his voice again

for his Elisabeth but you Dede—
Across your folded hands, I laid flowers
but all that life, once or twice, did I carry

proteas from the market?
Please come back, you love me
Ah! Leave me alone

I Arimis my face, jacket my chest, climb the road
to the shops. 80 shillings of goat, three-quarter sindano,
a hand of limes. I stop at Abdul's—you remember

him? Kimani's son? From the other side of the hill?
"Abdul, count my debts." The mason's account
is settled. Outside the hardware, TATA lorries

are painting Wambui's florist stand with dust.
The hill is almost a quarry now. A ferrier
swings a stick against a donkey's red ribcage.

The proteas! Is it summer again? In the square,
a mishikaki vendor's rag catches fire, is booted
into brown centipedes. It is summer again.

At Mama Rita's, felled podo trees are bandaged,
soaked and smoothed into cheapcheap "mahogany."
I show my back to Githinji's Bushere.

Past soda distributorships. The public school
where newly graduates are dusting off their hands,
where spades from Abdul's unearth latrines.

Dede, between here and home are three friends.
The tailor's legs are cramped. From new uniforms,
a weaning child learns they will join school.

Spoiled sheets are yanked from cold beds to air.
Turacos are circling the bougainvilleas again,
perching on the more purple branches.

Blueing the town again. Dede, on this other side
of the ground, it is summer again.
Won't you come back now?

I count one-, two-, and three-story mansions.
I cut through the plot next to ours
whose owners we never met.

The untrimmed keiapple. Burnt sixty-watts.
Rungs that need nails. It is summer again—
everything answerless as it was.

Kanda Bongo Man is soldiering
his hills-and-valleys voice through the bridge,
wailing, begging now—

> *My brother, leave that girl*
> *You know that she loves you just because of your money,*
> *Shut up! I love her*

Wole's whistling is the shadow driving
down the road, keying the mabati gate.
"Born Living, I was visited. My eyes say

you have cleaned your tongue without
me." I wear my laughing face, unzip
my mouth, make room for his tongue.

THE TEA DRINKER

She watches the sugar cube
starching the tea

how, desperately, it rises
tumbling up for air

and she knows
what she mustn't do.
Call again.

She stares at her Nokia
enticing it to ring.

She looks about
her room. Sooted
timber plastered

with newspapers.
Some so old, woven
into the house:

A firing squad
in Élisabethville.
A shooting in

Ougadougou.
Standoffs in Kashmir.
A police operation

in Algiers, Rio.
Aid trucks stuck
at Rafah.

She turns
the yellowed calendar
over to April.

Inside the radio,
The Nation reels:
"Hottest day on record."

"Opposition outlawed."
"Rebels advancing
in Congo, Sudan."

"Activists missing
in Uganda, Thailand,
Tanzania."

“Saudi, Indian, Russian
journalists dismembered.”
“American protesters

shot.”
“Civilian fishing vessels
decimated.”

“Migrants under
the Mediterranean.”
“Water still waiting

to cross Rafah.”
“Elections postponed.”
Speakers-down, she lays

her radio
on the windowsill.
Listens to the silence

of curfew. Wind
creaking the oak
and coiled nails.

Black tea sloshing
her stomach
to peaks and hollows.

KARATINA MARKET

He wears his mother's eyes each market day.
        She appraises the papayas, green oranges
rounding his thumb and forefinger. Go to
        the mud-wet pumpkin leaves at that stall.
Look—dirt or blight? He carries a palmful
        of iron beans to eyes that found fastest
where the roof leaked, keen for more than
        glimpses of *The Bold & The Beautiful*.
She watches as he knocks, asides the unripe
        melons. Baskets the least scabrous
tamarind. Jute, amaranth, bitterleaf.
        A breeze dusts the market.
He closes her eyes, private as a photo behind
        a photograph. He harrows his tongue
to haggle. A thin rasp sifts his throat as
        when one morning (cold light or fog),
watching a millet vendor, flour raining
        through a sieve quick & gone—
a remembered face parts the veil of life
        to stand among the butchered meats.
Each market has their own ghostroots.
        In this one, holding tight his other hand,
he may coax his dead lightward. He stows
        his bargains. The root-slashed cane,

a crop of red plums—everything ripens.

The wind that sheafs the reed is born of
the wind that bends the oak.

HARVESTS

Carl Philips's epigraph is from "No Kingdom" in *From the Devotions*.

Anne Carson's epigraph is from *Eros the Bittersweet*.

"To Spoon With You" is after Yu Xiuhua's gorgeous poem "Crossing Half of China to Sleep with You" translated by Ming Di.

"In Search of Wa Muthoni's Garden" takes its title from Alice Walker's *In Search of Our Mothers' Gardens*.

The epigraph by Mariama Bâ is from *So Long A Letter* translated by Modupè Bodè-Thomas.

In "Ode to the Heat of a Just-Vacant Seat," the poem engraved on a spaceship is a reference to Ada Limón's poem "In Praise of Mystery."

Roland Barthes's postgraph is from *Camera Lucida*.

"Ars Finis" is after El Anatsui's bottle top forms.

The form of "Ode to Dosa Man" is inspired by Namwali Serpell's story "The Account."

The form of several "Form-I-589" poems and "Elegy Lotioned to Ars Poetica," where the poem opens with an epigraph and ends with a postgraph, is inspired by African oral traditions where a story is not one person's creation but a communal endeavor. Creation is a journey with friends. I call this form Rafiki.

Fatimah Asghar's postgraph is from *If They Come For Us.*

"Ode to Incest Disguised as Litany" has a nod to Monica Youn's *From From.*

The epigraph and postgraph by Abraham Lincoln is referenced from the Library of Congress item "Abraham Lincoln papers: Series 1. General Correspondence. 1833–1916: Abraham Lincoln, Monday, February 11, 1861 (Farewell Address)."

The epigraph in part III is from Amos Tutuola's *Ajaiyi and His Inherited Poverty.*

In "Elegy Lotioned to Ars Poetica," James Baldwin's epigraph is from *Notes of a Native Son*, and Yusef Komunyakaa's postgraph is from "Ode to a Drum" in *Thieves of Paradise.*

Philip Larkin's epigraph in part IV is from "Days" in *Whitsun Weddings.*

In "The Door," the line "Death will wait" is from Gwendolyn Brooks's "To the Young Who Want to Die" in *The Near Johannesburg Boy and Other Poems.*

In "The Wake" is a glimpse of Miriam Makeba's and Harry Belafonte's "Malaika" in *An Evening with Belafonte/Makeba* (1965).

In "Endless Traffic," the epigraph by Bessie Head is from her letters in *A Woman Alone: Autobiographical Writings*, edited by Craig MacKenzie.

"The Sweet Keepers" is after Gwendolyn Brooks's "The Bean Eaters."

In part V, the epigraph by Zora Neale Hurston is from *Their Eyes Were Watching God*.

In "Ode to the Inviting Coldness of a Pillow," the quote by Thomas Jefferson is a reference to the "Thomas Jefferson, July 27, 1821, Autobiography Draft Fragment" in the Library of Congress.

Divya Victor's postgraph is from *KITH*.

"All the Way from There to Here" takes its title from Jack Gilbert's poem in *Monolithos*.

The poem "Ode to Kanda Bongo Man" spindles lyrics from Kanda Bongo Man's song "My Love Elisabeth" from his 1999 album *Sweet*.

GRATITUDES

Thank you to the readers and editors of the following publications where these poems appeared, sometimes in earlier versions:

Adi Magazine, Adroit Journal, Black Warrior Review, Callaloo, The Cincinnati Review, Copper Nickel, Gulf Coast, Michigan Quarterly Review, Obsididan: Literature and Arts in the African Diaspora, Orca: A Literary Journal, POETRY, Poetry Northwest, The Poetry Society of America, Qwani, West Trade Review.

I am grateful to the Pitt Poetry Series for believing in this project, and especially to Nancy Krygowski, Jeffrey McDaniel, Alex Wolfe, and Lesley Rains for their generous work, infinite patience, and support.

Thank you to my teachers. Such gratitude to Alice Liang, Gianna Improta, and Catherine Barnett for your guidance and fierce generosity throughout. I am grateful to Pumho Karimi and Vasvi Kejriwal for your generous confidence, to Oak Sikrom, Laetitia Keok, Clement Yue, Victor Muturi, Heather Kim, and Alishya Almeida for your nourishments.

I am grateful to my friends and dear family who make me possible. Thank you, Habib, for your unwavering being.

And thank you, dear Reader!